Be amazing...
always! :)

Jen

This book is dedicated to my nieces, nephews, and Godchildren who have inspired me and enriched my life in so many ways. I love all of you to the moon and back! May you each always dream brilliantly, and be the best you can be! I wish each of you to BE AMAZING!

Keara Lynn
Robert Samuel
Megan Elizabeth
Noah Jake
Kelsey Lynn
Grace Elizabeth
Leann Jennifer
Jonah Christopher

Author proceeds from this book will be used to create a college scholarship fund in the name of my angel nephew whose life ended way too soon. My beautiful nephew, Levi Alexander Benson, was nearly three months old when his life was cut short after the horrific illness, pertussis. Although only an infant, this little guy touched the lives of many. The scholarship will be called ***Levi's Legacy***, as a way for his memory to live on. You are always in our hearts sweet baby…

–Jennifer Gervase Benson

www.mascotbooks.com

The Three Little Girls and The Magical Unicorn

For more information, please contact:
Mascot Books
560 Herndon Parkway #120
Herndon, VA 20170
info@mascotbooks.com

CPSIA Code: PRT0914A
ISBN-13: 978-1-62086-821-8

Printed in the United States

The Three Little Girls
and
The Magical Unicorn

Written by

Jennifer Gervase Benson

Illustrated by

Theresa Stites

Once upon a time, there were three little girls.
They each wore their hair in pigtails with long brown curls.

The three little girls were two sisters named La-La and Furry, and a cousin named Flower.
When they were all together, they had a very special power.

Not power like superheroes…but the power of family.
They always shared a special bond that made them smile with glee.

When they were together, they giggled and laughed and ALWAYS had fun.
They played make-believe, went on trips, baked cookies, and frolicked in the sun.

Furry was the youngest, and a few years after she was born,
she would tell La-La and Flower about her Magical Unicorn.

They would tease her and say, "Unicorns aren't real; you have your head in a cloud."
Furry would just smile, but never commented aloud.

Belief in her Magical Unicorn
got her through many a scary time.
Throughout her life, when things got overwhelming,
her belief allowed her overcome it and find a way to climb.

Furry believed that any time she was afraid of something,
her Magical Unicorn would make it go away.
And as we all know, we are all faced
with fears each and every day.

Fear can be that feeling in your stomach or head
before a quiz in math or a performance in a play.
Fear happens when you play a soccer game, try something new,
or when you tell your mom you broke her favorite tray.

Any time Furry had a fear, she would just close her eyes and dream.
She would imagine riding on her unicorn and jumping over a rainbow's beam.

She would say to herself, "My unicorn isn't afraid, so neither am I."
And before she knew it, her fear went bye-bye.

She would watch her unicorn dance, flip, and do crazy eights on the lawn.
And lo and behold, what happened to her fear? *POOF!* Gone…gone…gone.

Her fear went away, because the unicorn was not scared.
And soon enough, because Furry believed in what her unicorn did, that lack of **fear** was now shared!

The three little girls each had favorite hobbies:
La-La loved to cook, Furry loved to draw, and Flower loved to garden.
Spending time doing those activities
always made them grin.

Flower absolutely loved flowers like daisies, lilies, tulips, and even the rose.
She knows everything about all of them; just ask her, Flower knows!

One day at school, Flower's teacher announced a huge city-wide art fair.
Flower wanted to enter and create a floral masterpiece, but the thought of it was more than she could bear!

She was so afraid and overwhelmed. *What if I lose?* she thought.
What if people laugh? What if it's not good enough? She became SO overwrought.

She knew that other kids would be making beautiful arts and crafts, murals, paintings, and ceramics.
The competitive spirit created WAY too many dynamics.

Later that afternoon, Flower was playing with La-La and Furry and told them about the art fair. She said, "I won't win anyways, why bother? I don't care!"

La-La said, "Flower, you HAVE to enter. Your creations are the best!"
And what happened next? Well, you might have guessed!

Furry reminded Flower of her Magical Unicorn for those times that are scary.
Just close your eyes and dream…and you will become less wary!

So Flower imagined her unicorn dancing and flying, and flinging beautiful flowers through the air.
Her unicorn spun and spun, creating a floral masterpiece to be showcased at the art fair.

In Flower's mind, she imagined her unicorn entering the competition.
In her mind, her unicorn actually had fun and EVEN WON!

Flower decided, *I am not afraid! If my Magical Unicorn can do it, so can I!*
And with that thought, she darted off quicker than a blink of an eye.

She began gathering all of her favorite flowers, ribbons, and other decoration.
And spent hours and hours assembling her masterpiece with huge admiration.

La-La and Furry helped Flower to carefully carry it to school on the day of the competition. The two sisters rooted for their cousin, and cheered and smiled. In their minds, she had already won!

After hours of the judges' viewing, scoring, and writing down their notes,
the time had come when they cast their votes.

Finally, the judge announced, "Flower, you won first prize!"
The three little girls screamed with joy, and La-La and Furry watched their cousin's gleaming eyes.

Flower ran to the stage, and collected her trophy. And as she did, she whispered, "I can do anything!"
She realized that when she believed in herself, how much magic it could bring!

The moral of the story is a very special lesson in belief.
When it comes to fear, we need to turn a new leaf.

What this means is to not let fear stop us.
When we are scared, it limits us and creates too much of a fuss.

Each of us must have HOPE, FAITH, and BELIEF to find a better way.
We must remember that tomorrow will always bring us a brand new day!

Face your fears, hop on your unicorn, and take it for a ride.
And before you know it, victory will soon be on your side!

Remember, there is no such thing as "I CAN'T"…only "I CAN!"
And it starts with a belief in yourself that guides you to your plan!

Hurray for your unicorn!
Your dreams can be born!

The End

Note to the Reader

This is the first book in *The Three Little Girls* series. Each book in the series will have a valuable theme and message for children. To send comments or inquire about upcoming books, please send an email to gervasebensonbooks@yahoo.com

About the Author

Jennifer Gervase Benson resides in Rochester, New York with her husband, Christopher, and dog, Bella. Although not blessed with their own children, Jennifer and Chris have several nieces, nephews, and Godchildren whom they love to spoil and spend their time with. Jennifer has a bachelor's degree in psychology and a master's degree in clinical social work. She currently works in corporate training and leadership development.

Turn that Frown Upside Down and *The Magical Unicorn* are two simultaneously published books by Jennifer. Both books are the first of two separate children's book series: *Bella's Adventures* and *The Three Little Girls*.

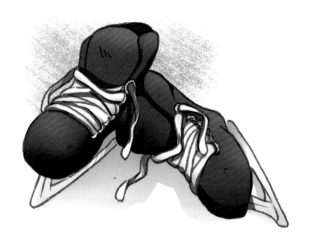

I would like to dedicate this book to my parents, for their
continued love and support in helping a boy work to follow
his dreams. I would also like to thank my wife, for
helping me share my story and make this book a reality.

Printed and bound in Canada
Published by Momentum Books, L.L.C., a subsidiary of Hour Media, L.L.C.
5750 New King Drive, Suite 100
Troy, Michigan 48098
www.momentumbooks.com

ISBN-13: 978-1-938018-09-1
LCCN: 2018955784

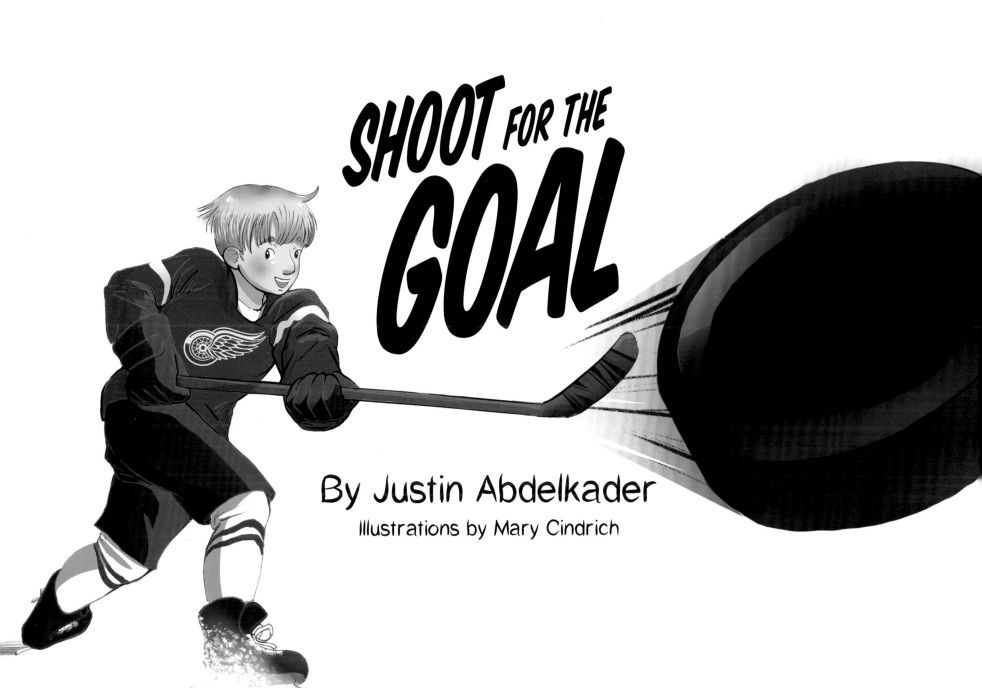

SHOOT FOR THE GOAL

By Justin Abdelkader

Illustrations by Mary Cindrich

When Justin turned 4,
he received his BEST.
BIRTHDAY PRESENT. EVER.

"My VERY OWN hockey jersey!"

CLICK SNAP

"You have some growing to do before it fits," Justin's mother chuckled.

Justin wore the jersey everywhere.

To preschool.

To eat dinner.

To bed.

He never wanted to take it off.

All he could dream about was becoming a hockey player.

Justin's dad took him to watch the older kids skate on Muskrat Lake. First they had to make sure the ice was safe.

"Frozen solid!" his dad said.
"Let's go!" the other kids shouted.
"Can I go out there, Dad?" Justin pleaded.
"You have to learn to skate first!"

To practice, his family went skating at the rink every Sunday. Justin pushed a chair on the ice, around and around, feeling more comfortable on the thin blades of his skates.

When Justin joined his first hockey team, his dad was one of the coaches. Justin loved it when his dad tied his skates and gave him a pep talk before each game.

When Justin was 8, his parents surprised him with tickets to his first Detroit Red Wings game.

"I can't wait to go!"

"You've got to get your science project done first," his mom said.

It took Justin's family three hours to drive to Detroit.

At the arena, Justin said, "One day, I'll be skating on this ice. I am going to be a Red Wing."

As Justin got older, hockey became a bigger part of his life. He practiced after school — even on the weekends. He did homework on the many long drives home from games. If he hoped to play hockey, he had to get good grades.

Justin decided to work as hard as he could. He kept practicing, day after day. Long after all the other players went home, he was still on the ice, shooting one puck after another into an empty net.

BANG!
THWACK!
WHACK!

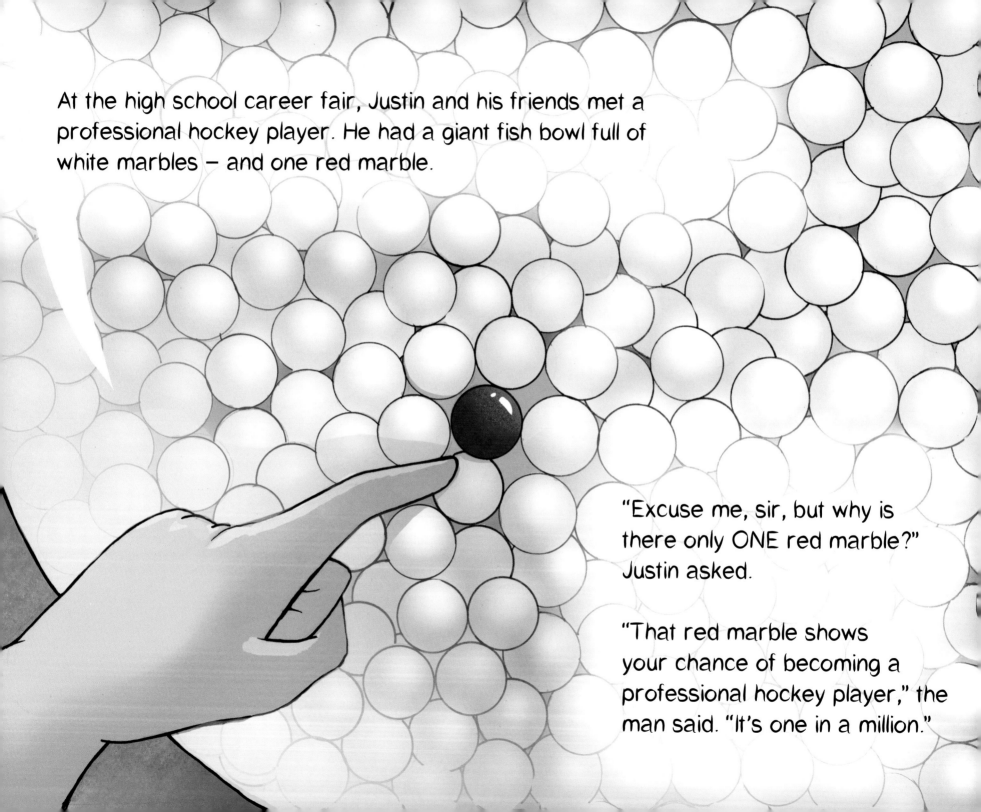

At the high school career fair, Justin and his friends met a professional hockey player. He had a giant fish bowl full of white marbles – and one red marble.

"Excuse me, sir, but why is there only ONE red marble?" Justin asked.

"That red marble shows your chance of becoming a professional hockey player," the man said. "It's one in a million."

At first, Justin was discouraged. Then he decided he would be that one red marble.

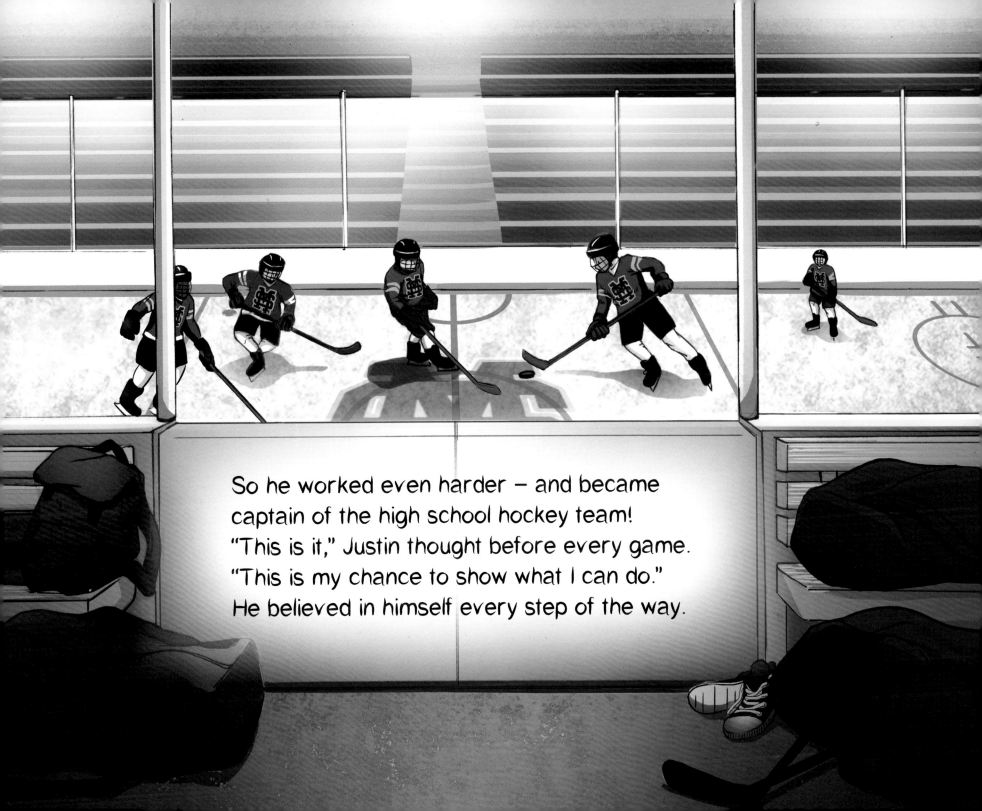

So he worked even harder – and became
captain of the high school hockey team!
"This is it," Justin thought before every game.
"This is my chance to show what I can do."
He believed in himself every step of the way.

Coaches from many colleges wanted Justin on their teams. But his heart was set on going to the same college his dad and grandpa had attended. He had pictured playing there his entire life. When he was offered a scholarship and a place on the team, he was thrilled.

One day Justin got the most exciting phone call of his entire life. It was the Detroit Red Wings. They wanted him to join the team. Did he want to? "OF COURSE I DO!"

He called his parents. They were happy, too, though it meant he would have to leave school before he could graduate.

"Promise me you will finish college someday," his mom said.

"I will."

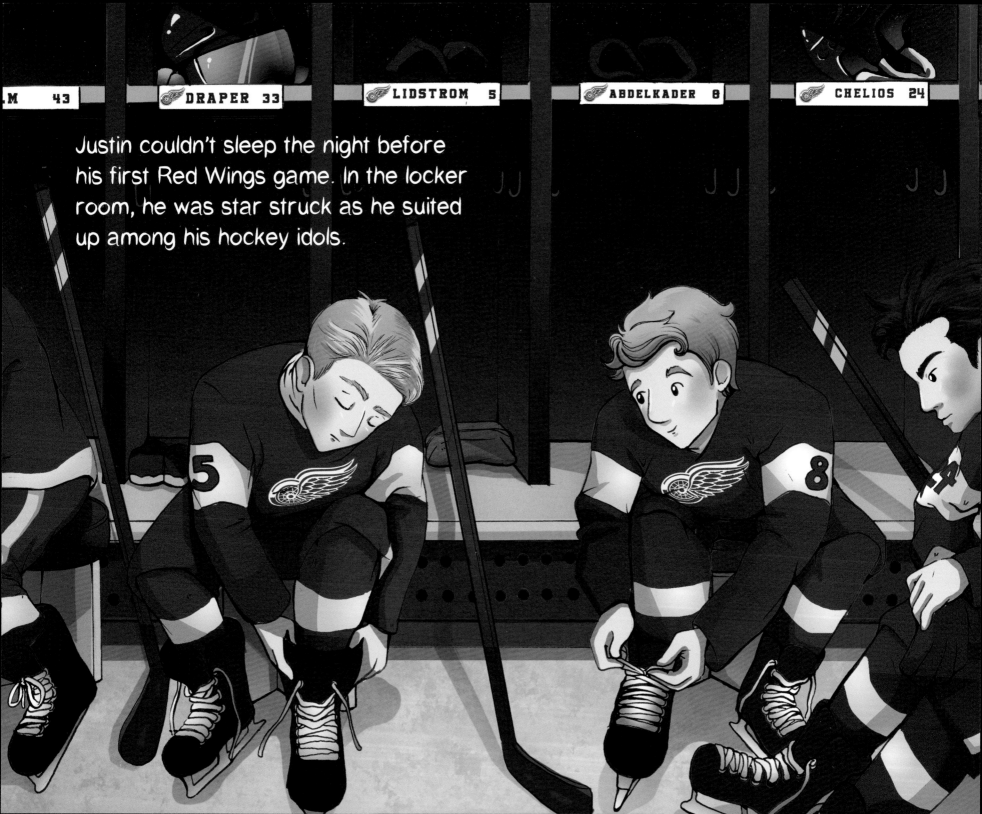

Justin couldn't sleep the night before his first Red Wings game. In the locker room, he was star struck as he suited up among his hockey idols.

When he skated onto the ice at Joe Louis Arena for the first time, the place was packed. The fans were on their feet. He knew he would remember this day for the rest of his life.

The Red Wings won the Stanley Cup that season! As Justin skated around the arena, he thought about the path that led him there. It had been a lot of work, but it was all worth it. It was the best feeling in the whole world!!!

Justin didn't forget his promise to finish college, either. It took a few years, but he finally earned his degree.

Justin had achieved his goals. He had become a professional hockey player! He had finished college!

"Stay with it," he tells kids now. "Work hard. Keep believing in yourself. Dreams do come true."

Justin Abdelkader was born to Sheryl and Joe Abdelkader in Muskegon, Mich., on Feb. 25, 1987. As a kid growing up on the west side of Michigan, he discovered his love for ice hockey and the Detroit Red Wings.

While attending Mona Shores High School, Justin was named captain of the high school hockey team and earned several honors including being named Michigan's Mr. Hockey in 2004.

Determined to become an NHL player, he made the tough decision to leave home during his senior year of high school and play junior hockey. He joined the Cedar Rapids Rough Riders and went on to win the 2005 Clark Cup.

Later that year, Justin committed to Michigan State University to play on the varsity ice hockey team. In 2007, Justin scored the game-winning goal in the NCAA championship game and earned the title of Frozen Four's Most Outstanding Player.

Justin was drafted 42nd overall by the Detroit Red Wings in 2005. After spending three years at MSU, he joined the Red Wings. Detroit then went on to win the 2008 Stanley Cup. Justin is currently in his 11th year with the organization and serves as the Red Wings' alternate captain.

He proudly earned his bachelor's degree in business from Michigan State University after years of taking classes in the off season. Justin is passionate about the importance of education for youth, and he helps act as a mentor for education through his Abby's All Stars reading program. Justin lives in Bloomfield Hills, Mich., and spends his summers in his hometown of Muskegon with his wife, Julie. They had their first child in September 2018.